PANCHTANTRA

Educative Stories

A marvellous collection of educative, entertaining and moral stories for children.

Compiled by : **Barratt**
Artworks : **Harvinder Mankad**

RAJA POCKET BOOKS
330/1, Burari, Delhi-110084

CONTENTS

New Edition : 2012

- **Panchtantra : Educative Stories : Barratt**

Publishers :
Raja Pocket Books
330/1, Burari, Delhi-110084
Tel. : 27611410, 27612036, 32938774, 27611227, 9582646426, 9582646427
e-mail : sales@rajcomics.com
website : www.rajapocketbooks.com

Showroom & Wholesale Outlet :
Raja Pocket Books
112, Ist Floor, Dariba Kalan,
Delhi-110006
Tel. : 23251092, 23251109, 32500860

Aditi Print-O-Fast
D-55, Secter A-5 & 6
Industrial Area
Tronica City, Loni
(Ghaziabad)

THE ADVICE OF AN ENEMY

There was a very big tree on the bank of a river. That tree was the home of a big flock of flamingos. A black snake lived in a hole near the roots of that tree. The snake used to eat flamingo chicks whenever they strayed away from their parents. This had been going on for years. The flamingos would not leave that place because the river was full of turtles, the favourite food of the flamingos.

Once, a father flamingo saw the snake eating away its young one. Now he knew, what had been happening to his earlier chicks. He was in deep grief. The tears rolled down from his eyes. A turtle saw this and asked, "Big uncle, why do you weep?"

When someone is in sorrow he readily tells his story to others. This lessens the burden of sorrow. So, the

flamingo told the turtle how the snake had eaten all his chicks and sobbed, “I wish to take a revenge.”

The turtle thought, ‘So, that is why you big uncle weep, huh ! When you eat our young ones then you do not spare any thought for us, the turtle parents. We too wish to take revenge on you.’

It was a mistake on the part of the flamingo to tell his misery to an enemy. The crafty turtle had already thought of a plan to kill two birds with one stone. The turtle spoke, “Big uncle, I can tell you a clever way of settling scores with that evil snake.”

The flamingo asked impatiently, “Tell me what is that. I will be thankful to you always.”

The turtle smiled in his heart and replied, “There is a burrow of a mangoose some distance away. You know that it is deadly enemy of snakes. The mangoose loves fish. You toss small fish on the ground so as to make a trail of the fish from the burrow of the mangoose to the home of the snake. The mangoose will reach to the snake eating the fish laid by you. Then it will kill the snake."

The flamingo said, "Show me the burrow of the mangoose, please."

The turtle obliged. The flamingo did as he was advised by the turtle. It happened just like the turtle had said. The mangoose reached the snake's hole eating the fish. Faced with the enemy, the snake hissed. In a short time the mangoose killed the snake.

The flamingo jumped up in victory. The turtle chuckled, "This is the beginning, idiot flamingo. Now my revenge starts. You flamingos will perish."

The turtle was right. The mangoose did not leave after killing the snake. It saw flamingos all over that place. The food for him for months. The mangoose made the same hole his home, in which the snake lived. He began hunting the flamingos. In a period of some time, all the flamingos became the meals of the mangoose.

Moral : The advice of an enemy has his own interest hidden in it.

THE DONKEY ROLL

There was a washerman in a town. He had a donkey on whom he carried the load of dirty clothes to the river bank to wash and then back. The washerman had a large family. His entire income went into feeding the family. Nothing was left for the fodder for the poor donkey. There was a pasture but only the cattle were allowed there. Shepherds drove away the donkey with sticks if it ever went there.

So, the donkey had grown very weak. Now the donkey could only travel very slowly taking double the time to cover the same distance as before. It worried the washerman too.

One day, when the washerman had spread the clothes to dry, a storm came. All the clothes got blown away. They had to be picked up from far and wide.

The washerman looked inside the tall grass also

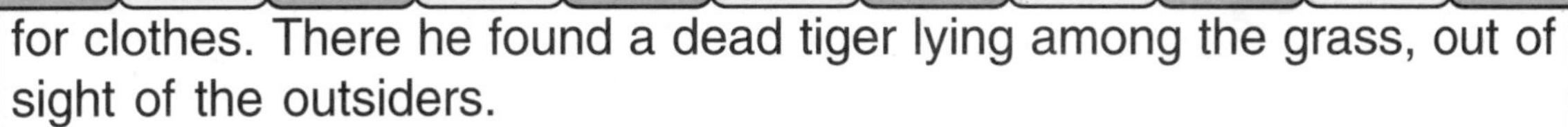

for clothes. There he found a dead tiger lying among the grass, out of sight of the outsiders.

The washerman returned with clothes. The donkey staggered as he tried to load the bundle of clothes on it. The washerman realised that the donkey will be too weak to carry any load in a few days. The worried washerman got thinking. A crafty idea came to his mind, "If I skin the tiger it might prove useful. I can put the tiger skin on the donkey and drive it into the fields at night. The people will be frightened away. The donkey would graze the crops and become healthy."

He did like wise. The next day, he went into the tall grass and skinned the tiger. He brought the hide home hidden among the washed clothes.

At night, when all went to sleep, the washerman dressed the donkey in tiger skin. The donkey looked like a tiger from a distance. He was satisfied. Then he drove the donkey into the fields. The donkey started grazing the field. When the farmers, guarding the crops, saw a tiger they ran away. The donkey had a hearty feast and returned home before the dawn broke. The washerman quickly removed the tiger skin and hid it. Now the donkey was happy.

Every night it would go to the fields wearing the tiger skin. Taking the donkey to be a real tiger the farmers stayed away and it ate the tender crops to his heart's content. The donkey became strong and healthy very soon. It carried heavy loads which made the washerman also happy.

As the days went by, the donkey grew stronger and fearless. That made it careless as well. One night, after having a bumper feast it decided to have a joy-roll just like asses and horses do when they are in happy mood. The donkey rolled on the crops. It rolled good many times. That felt so good. But in the process the tiger skin fell off. The donkey rose up in his true donkey form. One farmer had heard the snapping and crushing sounds made by the plants when the donkey rolled on them. He quietly came out to see the reason and found the donkey and the cast off tiger skin.

He yelled, "Hey! It is a donkey !"

The other farmers heard him. They all rushed there with big sticks. Meanwhile the donkey was about to bray. But before he could do that, stick blows rained on it. The donkey fell down and was beaten to death. The washerman who played this dirty trick had to leave the town.

Moral : You can not fool all the people all the time.

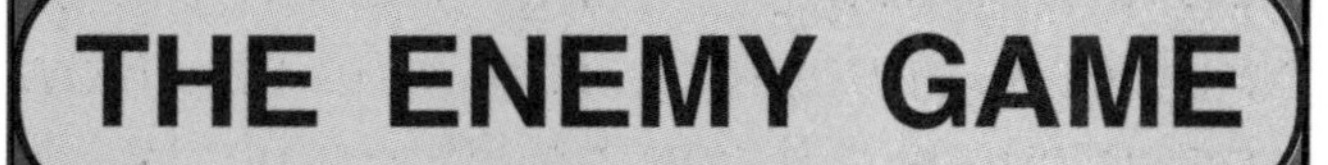

THE ENEMY GAME

Once there lived an old snake named Mandavisha in a hole near a mountain. In his youthful days he was a dreadful snake feared by all. He used to move like a streak of lightening. But the old age changes everything. Now Mandavisha was weak and moved very slowly. His fangs had become shaky like nails in rotting wood. The hissing made it huff and puff. The rats jumped over his body taunting him. Even catching slow moving creatures was becoming very very difficult.

Mandavisha's mind was still alert. He thought hard to find a way to get easy food. One day he hit upon an idea and went to Dadur pond. Dadur pond was a kingdom of frogs. Mandavisha creeped around the pond. Then, at a place, he saw the king of frogs basking in the sun on a large rock. Mandavisha saluted him by dipping his head and said, "Long live the great king of frogs."

The frog king was surprised, "You! You are our deadly enemy. Why do you hail me?"

Mandavisha replied politely, "O King. it is an old story. I acted like your enemy when I was young fool. That was sin. Now I want to wash my sins. I have been cursed. It can be lifted only by serving the frogs. My *guru* has so advised."

The frog king asked, "What curse you talk about?"

The crafty snake made up an imaginary story, "O King, once I was creeping around in a garden where some human children were playing. A child stepped on me by mistake. I bit the child and he died. Then I saw Lord Krishna in my dream. He put a curse on me which will turn me into stone figure by the end of this year. My *guru* told me that the death of the child, I bit, had angered lord Krishna as children are his own forms. I fell at his feet and asked what I could do. He took pity on me and revealed that if I gave the frogs joy rides on my back till the end of the year, the curse would be lifted. Please give me chance, O great frog king."

The frog king was really amazed at hearing this. What frog has ever got fantastic chance of riding a big poisonous snake? He thought that it would be wonder of wonders. The frog king leapt into the water. He told

all the frogs about Mandavisha story. The frogs were stunned. An old frog croaked, "Frogs riding a snake would be a great thing. We shall be hailed as the greatest of all the frogs."

The frogs lost their senses at the exciting thought of riding a great snake.

All the frogs agreed to take the golden chance. So, the frog king came out and spoke to waiting Mandavisha, "Well snake, we accept your offer."

So, seven or eight frogs jumped on the back of the snake. The king occupied the front seat and the grand joy ride began. After giving the frogs a jolly ride, the snake returned to the bank of the pond. At Mandavisha's request, the frogs dismounted from his front side. So, the king got down

first. The vily snake gobbled up the last frog who hopped down his head. Thus, it went on. After every joy ride the snake would swallow down the last one in a quick move. Mandavisha enjoyed it.

One day, an another snake saw him carrying frogs. He rebuked Mandavisha, "Fie on you! Don't you feel ashamed?" Mandavisha replied, "It is better than dying of hunger. When the body is old and weak, the mind is the only weapon left. There are no choices."

So, Mandavisha carried on his joyride business. He no more had to stay hungry. Gobbling up the last frog was becoming a great fun for him. The population of frogs was becoming less and less, as more and more frogs went into his belly.

One day, the puzzled frog king wondered, "I feel that there are much less frogs here than they used to be. I do not know why?"

Mandavisha explained, "O great frog king, your fame is spreading far and wide as the only frog king who rides a big snake. The frogs are going to other ponds and lakes to sing the praises of your greatness."

The stupid frog king believed it. His chest expanded with pride. Now the frogs becoming fewer and fewer did not worry him. In fact it pleased him. He thought he was becoming famous all over the world.

At last, the day came when all the frogs were eaten up. The king frog found himself alone sitting on the back of the snake. The king said sadly, "Is there no one left? How shall I live alone?"

Mandavisha smiled, "Do not worry, O great frog king. You shall not be alone. I will send you where others of your kind have gone."

So saying, the snake gobbled up the great king of frogs two.

Moral : Do not play in the hands of your enemy.

THE WISE JACKAL

Once upon a time, a lion stepped on a thorn. The thorn went deep into the paw. The paw hurt badly and it began swelling. The lion could not walk properly. The hunting became impossible because it takes a lot of running. For many days, the lion could hunt nothing and it went hungry. It had to eat something to stay alive. So the lion dragged itself around looking for some dead animal. Unfortunately no dead animal came in its sight. The hunger was becoming too painful.

The lion kept moving around hopefully. Then, at one place it saw a cave. It had a narrow mouth making it the kind of cave which serves as a den of wild animals. The lion peeped in. It was empty. There were signs all around showing that some animal lived in that cave. At that time the animal was out, perhaps, looking for food. The lion hid in the cave to kill the animal when it returned.

In fact, a jackal lived in that cave. It used to leave the cave in the morning and returned in the evening after spending the day out. On that day also, it came back after the sun had set.

The Jackal was very clever. It remained alert always. It saw paw marks of a big cat near the cave. It guessed that some lion or tiger might be lying in wait for him in the cave. The Jackal played a clever trick to check it out. It went a little away and called loudly, "Mister Cave! O Mister Cave, why don't you speak?"

There was silence. The Jackal shouted again, "Mister Cave, why don't you answer?"

The lion lay quietly inside. Its stomach rumbled with hunger. It was just waiting for the Jackal to come in, so that it could pounce on it. The lion was losing patience.

The Jackal called yet again, "Mister Cave, When I come, you always welcome and call me inside. Why are you silent today? I have already told you that the day you do not call me inside, I would leave you. So now I go to some other cave. Good bye."

This upset the lion very much. It thought that the cave really called the jackal in. To stop the jackal from going away the lion said in a gruffly voice, "Dear Jackal, I welcome you. Do come in, please. Do not go away. I have been waiting for you."

The Jackal at once recognised the voice of the lion. It walked away laughing at the foolishness of the lion. The foolish lion died of hunger in the same cave.

Moral : The alert ones do not get deceived.

THE CROWS AND THE OWLS

Long, Long ago, a giant banyan tree was the capital of crows. Thousands of crows swarmed it. Their king Meghvarna also lived on that tree.

There was a mountain nearby which had many caves of all sizes. Those caves were the homes of owls. Arimardana was their king. He was very brave and mighty. Arimardana hated crows. He called crows 'Enemy No. 1'. He was so hostile towards crows that without killing a crow he would not eat food.

When the number of crows getting killed each day increased, the king Meghvarna was alarmed. He called an emergency meeting of the crows and said, "Dear crows, you know that our lives have become very unsafe due to the attacks of the owls.

The enemy is powerful and knows no mercy. They swoop on us from above at night when we can not see. We can not counter attack during the day because they are safe inside dark caves at that time."

Then, Meghvarna invited the wise and the older crows to give suggestions.

A timid crow pleaded, "We must seek mercy of owls. We should accept whatever they ask of us. There is no sense in getting beaten up every day."

Several crows caw-caw'ed in protest. A haughty crow said, "We should not talk to the owls. Get up everyone and let us fight them."

A sad looking crow squeaked, "The enemy is very powerful. Let us leave this tree."

A wise crow suggested, "Leaving home is no good. If we go from here, we will break up. We must seek the help of other birds."

The wisest of all the crows, Sthirjeevi was silently listening to all.

The king Meghvarna turned towards him, "O wise Sthirjeevi, you say nothing. I want to hear your view."

Sthirjeevi spoke, "O King, when the enemy is strong, the deceit must be used."

"Deceit? What do you mean, Sir?" The king asked.

"Abuse me and attack me." Sthirjeevi advised.

The king Meghvarna was stunned, "What are you saying, Sthirjeevi?"

Shirjeevi hopped on to the branch the king was sitting on. He whispered in the King's ear, "We must put on this act. Many owl spies hidden in the trees nearby are watching our meeting . We should appear to be fighting among ourselves. Then you leave for Rishyamook mountain with other crows and wait for me. I will join the owls and plot their defeat. Please do as I say."

The act began. Sthirjeevi shouted loudly, "Stupid King, go and beg for friendship of the owls. Why do you ruin us?"

Several crows cried in protest, "Kill the traitor!" The king gave a nasty slap to Sthirjeevi with his right wing and threw him down. Meghvarna announced, "I declare Sthirjeevi a traitor. He is expelled from the crow family. He is an outcast. No crow shall have any dealings with him."

The spy owls perched on nearby trees watched this with glee. The king of owls was informed that the crows had fallen out and inside fighting had begun.

The commander of the owls suggested to the king Arimardana, "Sir, this is the right time to attack the crows. We will easily win the war."

Arimardana agreed with his commander. He ordered to launch the war at once. So, an army of thousands of owls swooped down on the crow tree making a frightening noise. The owls found no crow in that three. How could they? Because king Meghvarna had already left for Rishyamook mountain with all his crows. Finding the tree without any crow angered king Arimardana.He hatefully spat, "Fie on all the crows ! The cowards ran away instead of fighting with honour. A thousand shames on such cowards!"

All the owls hooted signalling their victory. Sthirjeevi crow watched it with satisfaction from a bush. He had fallen in that bush when his king had thrown him off the tree. He was carrying on the act. He crowed as if in pain. A spy owl saw him and said to the king, "Sir, that is the crow whom their king was slapping and abusing. He is down there in bushes."

The king Arimardana came down to the crow who looked in bad shape. He asked, "What happened, O Crow?"

Sthirjeevi sighed, "Ah Sir, I am no ordinary crow. I was minister of law to our king. I advised our stupid king to accept your leadership because we could not win war against the mighty king like you. This made our king angry. He rebuked me and expelled me from crow family. I seek your protection. Please take me under your wings."

The owl king thought deeply. A wise old owl advisor said in his ear, "Sir, the enemy should not be trusted. Order him to be killed at once."

A minister advised, "No sir, we must give him shelter. He will give us inside information on crows and tell us their secrets."

King Arimardana also thought likewise. He saw advantage in giving shelter to Sthirjeevi. So, the owls took him to their place. Arimardana said to his servants, "Sthirjeevi crow is our guest. Take him to the royal guest cave and look after him."

Sthirjeevi crow requested, "O great king, I feel very honoured. But let me stay on this rock, outside the royal cave. I just want to live like a humble servant and sing your praises."

So, Sthirjeevi made that rock his home.

The old wise owl protested, "Sir, giving shelter to the enemy in our own home is very dangerous. You are not doing right thing."

Arimardana angrily spoke, "Do not play smart with me. If you do not like my ways, you can go away." The old wise owl left the king along with some of his friends cursing.

A few days later Sthirjeevi started piling up twigs out side the royal cave saying, "Sir, the winter is coming. A little hut is needed to save me from cold."

Soon there was huge pile of dry twigs. One day when the owls were sleeping, Sthirjeevi flew away to Rishyamook mountain where king Meghvarna was waiting for him.

Sthirjeevi said, "Friends, a nearby forest is on fire. Pick a burning twig in your beak everyone of you and follow me."

An army of crows followed Sthirjeevi to the caves of owls. They were carrying burning twigs in their beaks. The twigs were dropped on the pile of twigs Sthirjeevi had collected. Soon, the flames leapt up. The owls died of burning or of suffocation as smoke filled the caves.

Moral : Do not shelter an enemy in your house.

THE BULL AND THE JACKALS

A farmer had a rogue bull. The bull would often go out of control to hurt other cattle of the farmer. The farmer was fed up with it. So, he turned the bull loose towards a jungle.

The jungle, where the rogue bull reached, was rich with green grass and tender bushes. It proved a heaven for the bull. Eating, stomping around and jostling with tress were the only things

he did. It became a picture of health and power. The bull turned into a huge bulk of muscles.

The mound on his shoulders grew into a giant bundle. The layers of skin hung down from his neck like garlands.

In the same forest, lived a pair of jackals. They would get a chance to eat only the left overs of the prey eaten by the big cats. They themselves could kill only small creature like mice or bandicoots. If lucky they might kill a lame rabbit once in a blue moon.

By chance, the bull happened to wander towards where the jackals lived. The bitch-jackal saw the bull and her eyes popped out. She called out to her husband and said, "Look at its muscles ! Imagine how tasty those would be !! A gift from God to us !!!"

The jackal sighed, "Quit the dreaming, wife. The bull's muscles and fat is no concern of ours."

The bitch-jackal flared up, "You are stupid. Can't you see the rocking bundle of big fat on its shoulders ? It will topple down any moment. We just have to pick it up. And the thick folds of meat hanging down by its neck will fall down any time. Let us follow it." The jackal advised, "Do not be so greedy, dear."

His wife insisted, "You are a coward. It is foolish to miss this chance. You must come with me. I won't be able to eat so much meat myself."

The jackal saw that his wife would not listen to him. So he gave up. Now they both started following the bull. The days went by. The bull shed no meat. The jackal tried to reason with his wife, "Come on, Let us go back. We can kill a few rodents to eat and stay alive."

But the bitch-jackal refused to see any reason. She huffed, "No. We shall eat only fat and juicy meat of this bull. Some day the meat will tumble down and we shall feast."

They went on following the bull. One day, too hungry and too tired to move any further, they tottered down to die of starvation.

Moral : Too much greed is no good.

THE POWER OF UNITY

Once upon a time, a flock of pigeons was flying in the sky looking down for food. It had strayed into a region which was facing famine. No food could be spotted. The leader of the flock was worried. Because the pigeons were fast tiring out. Something to eat was urgently needed to regain energy. The youngest pigeon of the flock was flying low to look for food on the ground and to inform the others.

After much flying, the area under the famine ended. They could see greenery down below. The youngest pigeon started flying lower hopefully. Then he saw a lot of food grains scattered in a field below. It informed the leader, "Uncle, I see food grains down below in a field. Enough food for all of us."

The leader at once ordered the flock to land in the field and feed on the grains.

The flock landed and began feeding.

The grains were in fact a bait put down there by a bird catcher. Upon a tree was his net, ready to fall down on the birds who took the bait. The net came down and trapped all the pigeons who were busy feeding.

The leader of the flock sighed, "Oh ! The food grains were to fool us. It was a trick. I should have guessed. I was too hungry to use my brain."

A pigeon wept, "It is the end of our story."

All the pigeons had given up hope. They waited for death. But the leader was thinking. Suddenly he spoke, "Listen, the net is strong. But it is not strong enough to match the power of unity. We can save ourselves by uniting our powers."

A young pigeon fluttered, "What do you mean by that, O wise one ? Please tell us in simple words. We stand divided by the net. How do we unite ?"

The leader explained, "All of you hold the strings of the net by your beaks. When I signal, all will fly in one move."

The pigeons did as they were ordered by their leader. Just then, the bird catcher appeared. His eyes brightened when he saw the flock of the pigeons trapped in his net. He tightened his hold on the stick he was carrying. And he ran towards the net.

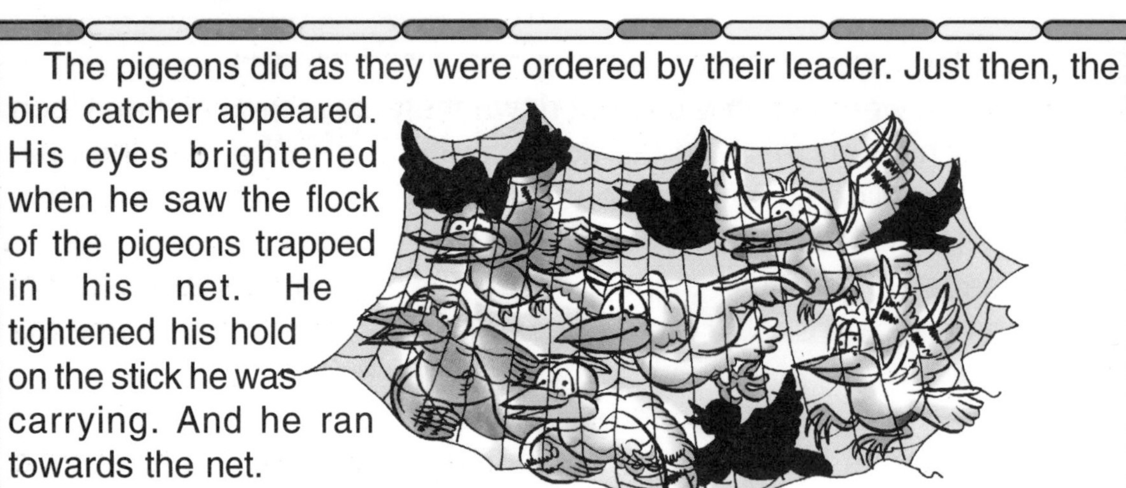

When he was merely a few steps away, the leader of the pigeons signalled, "Fly !"

In one united move the pigeons pushed up to fly. The entire net rose in the air and the pigeons began flying with it. The bird catcher looked up in disbelief. His net was being flown away. Then, he started running following the flying net.

The leader of the pigeons saw the bird catcher below following them. He knew why. The birds could fly like that only for a short time. Then the weight of the net would bring all of them down. But the leader had a solution for it. In the nearby mountain, the leader's friend mouse lived in a hole. The leader asked the pigeons to fly to that mountain fast. They landed with the net near the hole of the mouse.

The leader called out to his friend. When the mouse came out, the leader told him the story in brief. He asked him to nibble the net to set them free. The mouse nibbled the net fast and freed the pigeons. After thanking the mouse friend, the pigeons zoomed up to fly as free birds again.

Moral : United we can face the biggest problems.

THE CAMEL WITH THE BELL

Once there was a weaver in a village. He was very poor. He had been married when he was just a kid. The wife would one day move in to live with him. Then he would have to spend more money on the family. This always worried him. One year, no rains came. The people became poorer. No one could afford any new clothes. The weaver's income dried up. He was forced to move on to a nearby city to make both ends meet.The weaver did some menial jobs in the city. He saved some money. One day, he heard the news from the village that the rains had come and the situation was getting better. The weaver decided to return to his village.

On the way, he saw a sick cow-camel. She appeared to be pregnant. The weaver took pity on her and brought her along to his home. He took good care of her. She became healthy and gave

birth to a baby camel. The baby camel proved lucky for the weaver. A painter had come to the village to paint pictures of the village life. He would take the hair from the tail of the baby camel for his brushes. He went back after two weeks.

The cow-camel was giving enough milk. The weaver started selling the milk. The painter also returned to the village some time later. He had won many prizes on the pictures he had painted in the village and had made good money. The painter gave the weaver some money as thanks for the baby camel's hair he had taken for his brushes. The weaver bought a cute little bell for the baby camel with that money.

Now, the weaver had enough income to be able to bring his wife to his home. He was very happy now. Both the husband and the wife loved to see the baby camel run around playfully jingling his bell.

The camels proved so lucky for the weaver that he decided to become a camel trader. His wife also agreed with him. She was himself in a family waynow.

The weaver bought some camels and his camel business proved a great success. He had a large herd of camels now. Everyday, the camels would go to the pasture to graze. The weaver's baby camel had grown into a young camel. He would also go jingling his bell proudly keeping a respectable distance from others.

One day, another young camel asked, "Brother, why do you not come near us, the other camels? You always stay away from us. I have never seen you talking to another camel except you mother. Why so?"

The camel-with-the-bell boasted, "You are ordinary lowly

camels. I am like son to my master. I can not lower my position by getting mixed up with you."

A lion also lived near the pastures. He watched the camels from a high rock. The lion noticed that a camel kept aloof from the rest. To hunt, lions target such animals who are not part of a group or herd. And because of the bell this camel was inviting to be hunted. Because the sound of the bell could help the lion pounce on its target.

The next day, the camel-with-the-bell was keeping itself behind the rest of the camels by at least twenty camel steps. The lion was on the prowl. He targetted the sound of the bell and sprang. The lion landed on the neck of the camel-with -the-bell. It took seconds for the lion to finish the camel and drag its body into the bushes to eat.

Moral : One who considers oneself above one's own people pays a heavy price.

THE CLEVER JACKAL

There lived a very clever jackal in a forest. One day, he found an elephant who had fallen into a deep trench. The jackal sat above, waiting for the elephant to die. At night, the cool air gave strength to the elephant to get up and come out of the trench. But that was all it could do. It staggered again and fell down to die.

The jackal examined the dead elephant from all sides. The elephant's skin was too hard for the jackal to tear. There was no cut or tear anywhere through which it could try to reach the soft flesh. The jackal sat thinking. He must get some big cat to tear away the thick skin. And at the same time prevent it from eating the flesh. It was a tricky problem.

Then, he saw a lion coming that way. The jackal saluted the lion and spoke, "O great sir, this elephant was lying here dead. I thought that it

was fit for the king of the jungle to eat. So, I was guarding it for you. Sir, have a royal feast, please."

The lion growled, "Idiot, lions don't eat dead animals. We eat our kill only."

The lion went away. The jackal heaved a sigh of relief. A little later, a wolf walked in, looking hungrily at the dead animal. The jackal asked, "Uncle, are you thinking of eating it ?"

"Can you dare to stop me ?" The wolf thundered.

The jackal shrugged his shoulders, "I am no body to stop you. Go ahead. But it would be better if you don't."

The jackal whispered in the wolf's ear, "The king of the jungle, lion, has learnt that some superior animals like you have fallen low enough to eat dead rotting creatures. See the kite hovering above ? It is the King's spy watching who eats this dead elephant to report to the king."

The wolf looked up and saw a kite gliding above. The alarmed wolf did not stay there another second. Then, the jackal saw a cheetah passing by. He did quick thinking and approached the cheetah. "Good morning, prince Sir. I pay my respects." The jackal said bending down courteously.

The cheetah questioned, "What are you doing here, jackey?"

The jackal pointed to the dead elephant and spoke in low voice, "The lion killed it and left me to guard it."

"Oh !" The cheetah sighed and squeaked, "If it is lion sir's kill then I think I must go away quick."

The jackal called out to the departing cheetah, "O Prince sir, if you like elephant meat you are welcome to eat it."

The cheetah looked scared, "N..N..No..Jackey, No !"

The jackal said cunningly, "You need not worry, O Prince. I will tell the lion that a leopard ate the

elephant forcibly threatening to kill me. No problem."

The cheetah pounced on the elephant. In one move, it tore apart the elephant skin. Suddenly the jackal cried, "Oh, oh ! Prince sir, we are doomed."

Then he stammered, "He..he..here comes the lion !"

The cheetah looked shocked as if whipped hard. And he disappeared in one long leap. The clever jackal feasted on the elephant for several days.

Moral : The clever ones make others do what they want done.

THE BASIC NATURE

In a forest, there lived a *Mahatma*, a great sage. He had amazing divine powers. Every morning, he would come to the river to take bath and then meditate sitting a big rock for long hours. A hut among the trees was his home where his wife also lived.

One day, a strange thing happened. At the end of the meditation he always paid obeisance to God with folded hands. On that day, as he was bringing his palms together, a tiny female mouse landed in his palms. It so happened that a kite was flying overhead with that mouse in its clutches.

Somehow, the mouse escaping from its hold had fallen down. The sage looked at the frightened baby mouse.

The sage and his wife were childless. His wife always longed for a baby. The sage knew that his wife would never become a mother. It was so fated. But the sage never told this fact to his wife for fear of hurting her feelings. But he wanted to do something about it. A woman's life is fulfilled only when she becomes a mother. He knew this very well.

The female baby mouse trembling in his hands gave him an idea. He closed his eyes and chanted a powerful divine *mantra*. The power of *mantra* changed the baby mouse Into a human girl baby. The sage went to home holding that baby. Giving the baby to his wife, the sage spoke, "Dear, you always wished for a baby. The God has answered your prayers and has sent this girl baby. Bring her up as your own child."

The wife of the sage was overjoyed. She took the girl and kissed her saying, "Oh ! What a cute little cuddly baby ! My baby she is. I will treat her like one."

Thus, that baby girl became a part of the sage family. The wife of the sage named the baby 'Kanta'.

She showered mother's love and care on the baby. The sage also treated Kanta as his own child. They became so involved with Kanta that the fact of her being a female mouse ever was forgotten. It pleased the sage to see his wife cuddling and playing with Kanta.

At night, they would tell stories to Kanta until she did not fall asleep.

When the right time came, the sage began giving education to Kanta. She grew up playing, learning and basking in the warmth of the love of her foster parents. All the three were so very happy. The time went by. Kanta blossomed into a young lady of sixteen, beautiful and educated. The mother began thinking about the marriage of Kanta. One day she said to the sage, "Look, our Kanta is now a young lady. We must marry her off."

Just then, young Kanta came. She had a flower in her hair and her eyes were dreamy. The blush on her cheeks told the sage that his wife was correct. He whispered in the ears of his wife, "You are right. We shall seek out the most suitable groom for our daughter."

The sage, using his divine powers, invoked the Sun God. Sun appeared before the sage and spoke, "O sage, why did you call me ? What can I do for you ?"

The sage replied pointing towards Kanta, "This is my daughter Kanta. She is a worthy girl. I want you to marry her."

Kanta intervened, "Father, he is very hot and too bright. I won't be able ever to let him come near me or look at him."

The sage patted her on the back and said, "Alright. We shall find another groom. Still better."

Sun suggested, "O sage, the cloud is superior to me. He blocks my rays. Talk to him."

The sage invoked the Cloud god. Cloud arrived thundering and flashing the lightening. Kanta protested, "Father, he is too dark. I am fair skinned. We do not match."

The sage asked Cloud, "Who is better than you ?"

Cloud replied, "Wind. He blows me away."

The sage, now invoked the Wind God. They felt the presence of swirling wind. The sage turned to Kanta and questioned, "Do you like him, baby ?"

Kanta moved her head sideways. "No, father, he is too loose and does not stay at one place. No stability."

The wife of the sage also rejected Wind. "We can't give our Kanta to Wind. I would like to see my son-in-law with my own eyes. Wind is invisible."

So, the sage asked Wind, "What do you suggest?"

Wind murmured, "O sage, try Mountain. He stops even me."

On invocation of the sage, Mountain appeared there. Mountain said, "Why did you summon me, O sage ?"

The sage told him the matter. Mountain put a question, "Does your daughter approve of me?"

Kanta spoke, "Oh, he is all stone. I guess his heart is also made of stone."

The sage enquired from Mountain, "Tell me who is better than you ?"

Mountain said, "Mouse. It makes hole in me to live."

As he was saying this, a mouse jumped down from the ear of Mountain. On seeing the mouse Kanta became excited and squealed, "Father ! Father, I like this mouse. His ears and tail is cute. I want him. Let me marry this mouse, please."

With the power of *mantra*, the sage had transformed a female mouse into a human being but the basic nature remained that of a mouse. The sage again transformed Kanta into a female mouse and let her go with the mouse of her choice.

Moral : Artificial means can change outer appearance only. The basic nature of a creature remains the original.